God, You Are Always with Us

English text by

Carrie Lou Goddard

Illustrations by Kozo Kakimoto

Abingdon Press

It was very early in the morning.
The sun was rising. Its light
touched the many colors that God
has made. The yellows, the purples,
and the reds of the flowers, the
vegetables, and the fruits.
This was a beautiful new day.

The sunshine woke Mary and Jeremy. Jeremy stretched his arms and legs and bounced out of bed. Mary yawned, wiped the sleep from her eyes, and dressed herself.

"Let's go exploring," Jeremy said to Mary after their morning prayers.

"I'm ready," she answered.

Mary and Jeremy stepped out of the door. "Hello," Jeremy said to his dog, Brownie.

"You look surprised to see us," Mary said. "We are going to explore God's world. Would you like to go with us?"

Brownie wagged his tail.

"You must open your eyes very wide to see the world with us," Jeremy explained to Brownie. "Come along, let's go."

Jeremy, Mary, and Brownie walked along the garden path.

"Oh, look," Mary cried, "A yellow butterfly!"

The butterfly flew into the air. Jeremy and Mary and Brownie saw its golden wings against the blue of the sky.

"How beautiful!" Jeremy exclaimed. "I wonder what the butterfly sees as it flies through the air?"

"Can it talk to the wind that carries it up into the sky?" Mary asked. "Can it talk to God?"

Mary and Jeremy paused to listen to the wind. They heard its song whispering through the flowers. They wondered about the butterfly.

Jeremy turned to look at all the flowers. There were violets, tulips, pansies, daffodils, and many others.

"So many colors!" Mary cried as she looked at each of the flowers.

"Watch where you're going!" Jeremy called out to Mary. "You are about to step on an ant!"

Mary stopped and looked down. There was an ant on the garden path. Mary stooped down and watched as the ant hurried away.

"There are surprises everywhere," Mary said to Jeremy. "Up in the sky, growing in the garden, and close to the ground!"

Brownie wagged his tail.

Jeremy and Mary looked around and saw a cow lying in the grass. The cow looked at them with big brown eyes.

"What do you think the cow sees with her big brown eyes?" Mary asked.

"Oh, many things," Jeremy answered, "but mostly grass."

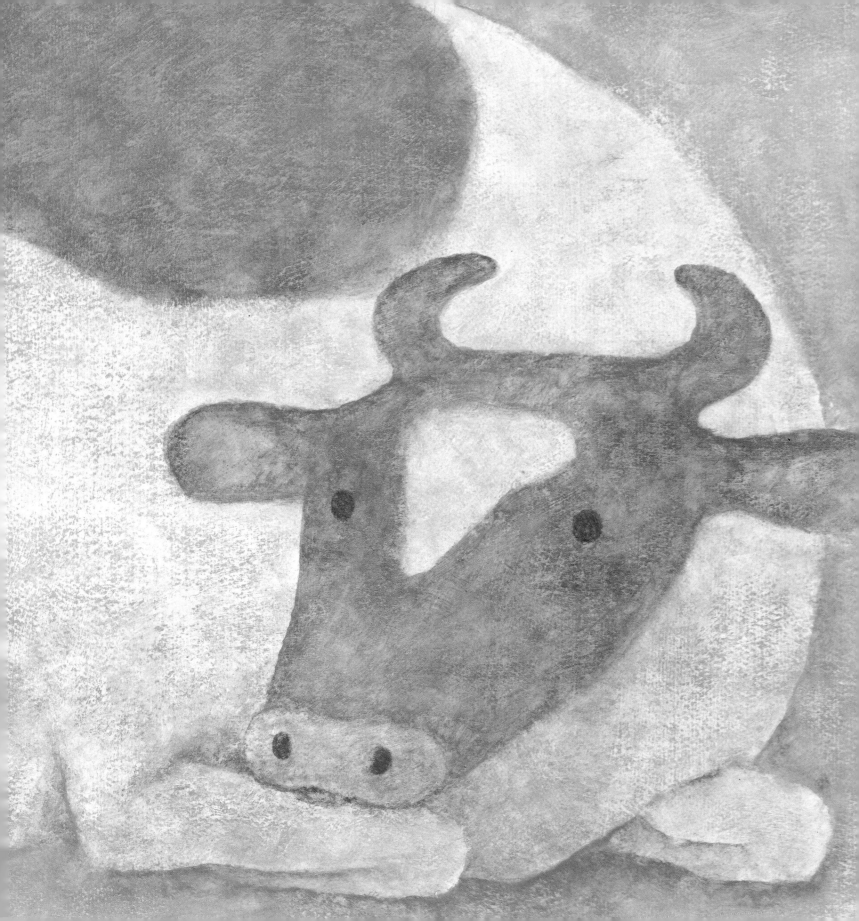

Jeremy and Mary turned back toward the garden. They saw a radish lying on the ground.

Jeremy picked up the radish. "It's darker on one side," he said.

Mary said thoughtfully, "Maybe the radish has been in the sun too long."

Suddenly Mary and Jeremy hear a rooster crowing.

"Wake up! Get up!" the rooster seemed to be saying. "See and hear what is happening in the world."

Brownie barked at the rooster.

In the center of the garden there was a pool of water. Jeremy and Mary stood on the edge of the pool. The water reflected their faces like a mirror.

"A fish!" Jeremy cried.

Mary looked where Jeremy was pointing. There was a fish swimming around in the water. The fish and the water looked green.

"There are surprises in the water, too!" said Mary.

Mary walked away from the pool. A flash of color caught her eye. It was the sun shining through drops of water clinging to a small twig.

"It looks like a rainbow!" Mary said.

"It is a tiny rainbow," Jeremy agreed, "but it is not like the big ones that come when it stops raining."

Jeremy, Mary, and Brownie walked through the garden gate. There was Mother and their baby brother.

"What did you find while you were exploring?" Mother asked.

Jeremy and Mary thought for a moment, then Jeremy said, "A yellow butterfly, flowers, and an ant, a cow with big brown eyes, a radish, a crowing rooster, and a swimming fish."

"A tiny rainbow and this bird sitting in my hand," Mary added. Mother smiled. "You have seen the many wonders which God created."

When the day ended, darkness came.
The stars shone in the sky.
It was time for bed.
Good night, Mary and Jeremy.
Have pleasant dreams while God watches over the world.

Printed in Japan

ISBN 0-687-15303-4